Search and Find
Space

Licensed exclusively to Top That Publishing Ltd
Tide Mill Way, Woodbridge, Suffolk, IP12 1AP, UK
www.topthatpublishing.com
Copyright © 2017 Tide Mill Media
All rights reserved
0 2 4 6 8 9 7 5 3 1
Manufactured in Zhejiang, China

Control center chaos

At the spaceflight control center they are busy monitoring the intergalactic scene. Can you find all the things listed?

Can you find?

1 moon

2 explosions

3 traffic controllers

4 guards

5 aliens with green heads

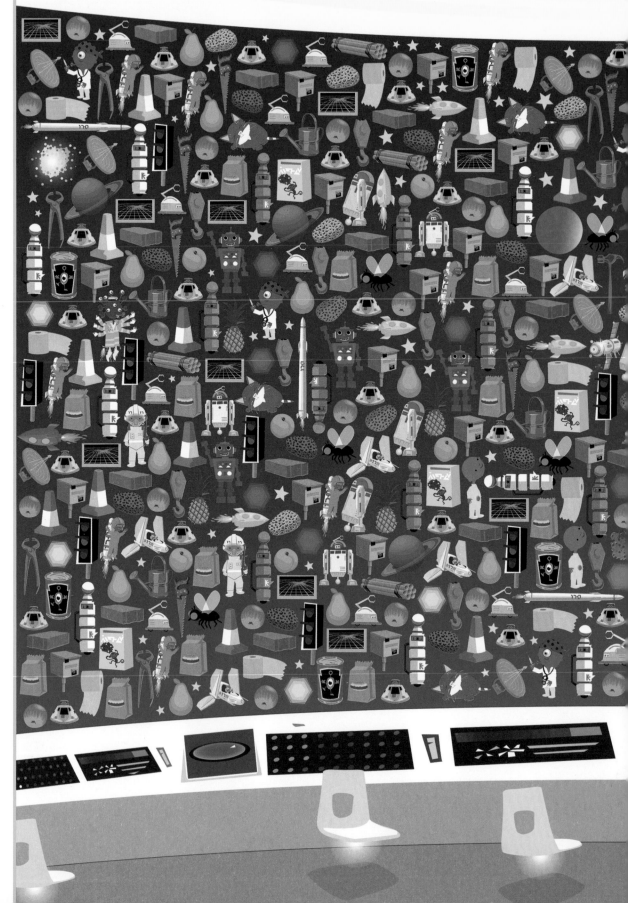

6 planets

7 space cats

8 cereal boxes

9 traffic cones

10 spaceships

1 receiver dish

2 alien spaceships

3 aliens with jetpacks

4 orange planets

5 planets with rings

Observation deck

The view from the observation deck is out of this world—literally! Can you find all the things listed?

Can you find?

6 space spiders

7 red planets

8 crew

9 explosions

10 spacefish

The loading bay

The loading bay at the space station is a busy place. There's always someone (or something) coming and going! Can you find all the things listed?

Can you find?

1 pink robot

2 red lights

3 oranges

4 pineapples

5 grabber cranes

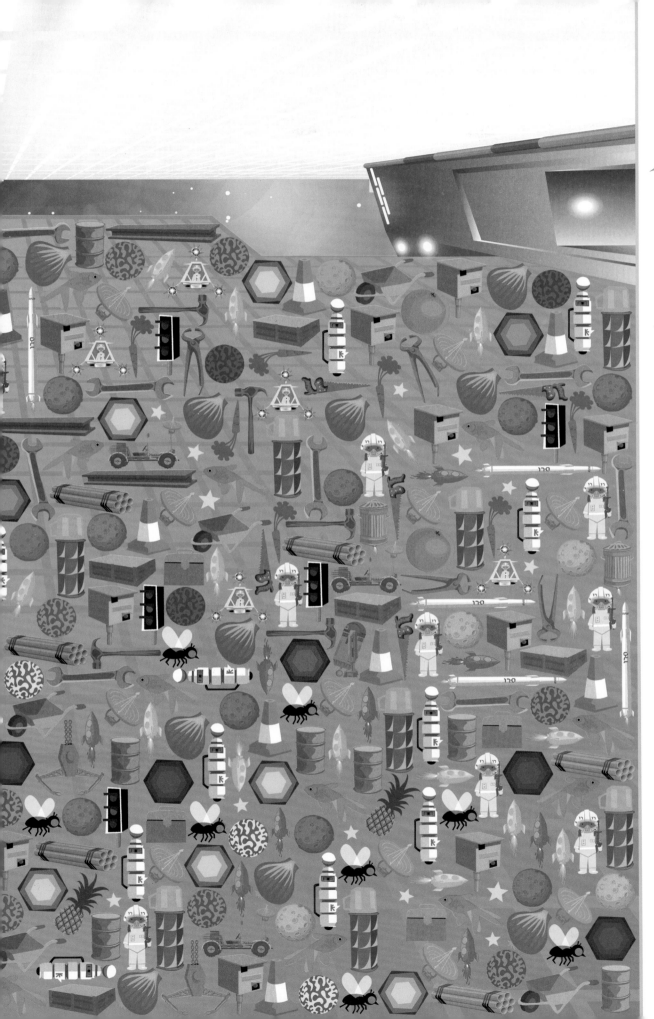

Can you find?

6 spaceships

7 moon buggies

8 rocket trash cans

9 space cargo crates

10 barrels

Can you find?

1 yellow taxi

2 fires

3 tanks

4 flags

5 explosions

Alien attack!

Uh-oh! Aliens have traveled to Earth and have started to attack! Can you find all the things listed?

Can you find?

6 helicopters

7 alien spacecraft

8 seagulls

9 soldiers like this

10 manhole covers

1 moon

2 red robots

3 grabber cranes

4 green robots

5 pink robots

Scramble interceptors

Alien spacecraft are approaching the space station and the space station interceptor craft have been scrambled. Can you find all the things listed?

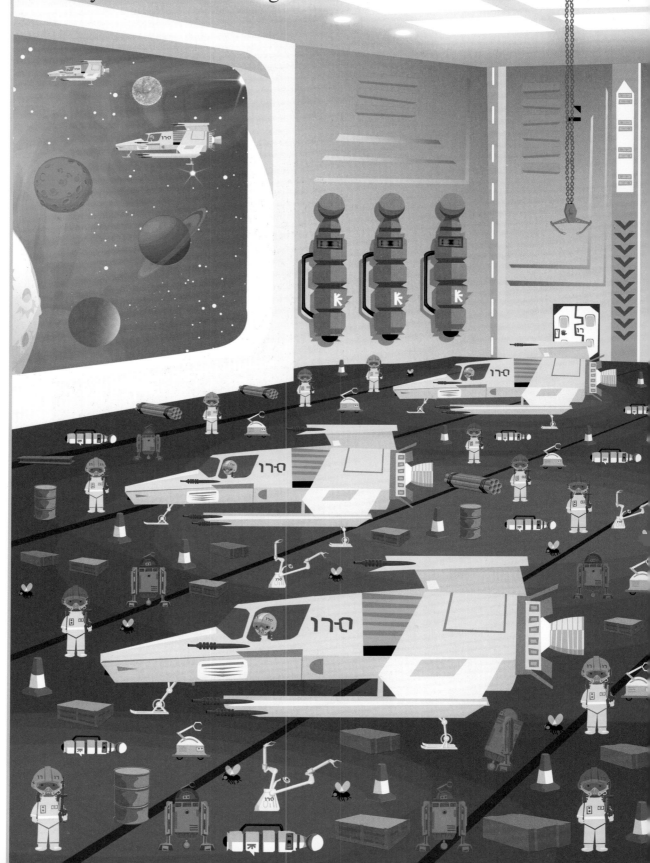

Can you find?

6 barrels

7 crew with
red helmets

8 spaceships

9 crew with
blue helmets

10 crew with
green helmets

1 moon

2 planets

3 space dragons

4 blue spacecraft

5 missiles

Look out!

As the space station pilots intercept the approaching craft, the aliens unleash all of their firepower!
Can you find all the things listed?

Can you find?

6 interceptor craft

7 alien craft like this

8 explosions

9 asteroids

10 rocket trash cans

Salute the heroes

The alien invaders have been defeated! As the triumphant interceptor pilots return to the space station, people line the viewing decks to congratulate them. Can you find all the things listed?

Can you find?

1 furry alien

2 yellow robots

3 black starships

4 blue robots

5 space bugs

Can you find?

6 red spaceships

7 yellow spaceships

8 satellites

9 blue spaceships

10 missiles

Can you find?

1 silly alien

2 rocket trailers

3 alien dogs

4 space harvesters

5 flying saucers

Planet Yoobee

Planet Yoobee is home to little green men who grow crops to make their favorite food—breakfast cereal! Can you find all the things listed below?

6 jars of alien eyes

7 red cereal boxes

8 yellow cereal boxes

9 turtle-toucans

10 alien farmers

1 broken down pod

2 purple dragons

3 blue cereal boxes

4 aliens like this

5 flying saucers

Space race

It's the annual intergalactic pod racing championship. Some of the fastest craft ever built are racing today. Can you find all the things listed?

**6 aliens
in carts**

**7 blue
aliens**

**8 aliens
like this**

**9 aliens
like this**

**10 oil
spills**

Can you find?

1 watermelon

2 watering cans

3 scientists

4 bunches of bananas

5 tanks of carrots

Giant biospheres

The space station is completely self-sufficient. Fruit, vegetables, and other crops are grown in giant biospheres. Can you find all the things listed?

Can you find?

6 grapefruit

7 faucets

8 tanks of potatoes

9 pineapples

10 bio robots

Can you find?

1 blue alien

2 drones

3 green bottles

4 moon buggies

5 red aliens

Explorers

Space scientists search the galaxy looking for new planets that can sustain human life. Can you find all the things listed?

6 guards

7 purple bottles

8 green robots

9 space rovers

10 red lights

1 pink planet

**2 signs
like this**

**3 aliens
like this**

**4 traffic
cones**

**5 orange
rockets**

Space mall

With its trendy shops and restaurants, this is
probably the coolest shopping spot in the galaxy!
Can you find all the things listed?

Can you find?

6 space
takeouts

7
milkshakes

8 blue
rockets

9 flying
saucers

10 drones

Can you find?

1 hammer

2 flasks

3 rocket trash cans

4 crane hooks

5 gun turrets

Repair dock

Spaceships need constant repair and updating. This vast hangar is being used to make modifications to a destroyer vessel. Can you find all the things listed?

Can you find?

6 crates of
space cargo

7 adjustable
wrenches

8 barrels

9 work
lamps

10 mechanics

1 satellite

2 traffic enforcement cameras

3 traffic controllers

4 craft like this

5 stop lights

Flying test

All children who live on board the space station must learn to fly small two-seater spaceships by the time they are ten years old. Can you find all the things listed?

Can you find?

6 drones

7 alien spaceships

8 pineapples

9 asteroids

10 two-seater spaceships

1 fry pan

2 trailers

3 flashlights

4 blue coolers

5 tents

Visit to Earth

This alien spaceship has paid a visit to Earth.
The aliens are beaming up a child to see if he wants to
watch a movie. Can you find all the things listed?

Can you find?

6 camping chairs

7 pairs of briefs

8 cans of beans

9 rolls of toilet paper

10 pails

1 flask

2 toolboxes

3 forks

4 people at work signs

5 hammers

Spacewalk search

While traveling close to an unknown planet, this starship was damaged by passing asteroids. It's the crew's job to repair the damage. Can you find all the things listed?

Can you find?

6 yellow spacecraft

7 rolls of toilet paper

8 explosions

9 wheeled robots

10 traffic cones

Fighter training fun

Flying a fighter craft is one of the greatest honors for a spaceship pilot. This squadron are preparing for take off. Can you find all the things listed?

Can you find?

1 guard like this

2 jetpack pilots

3 yellow traffic cones

4 moon buggies

5 blue wheeled robots

Can you find?

6 blue guards

7 red robots

8 milkshakes

9 drones

10 red pilots

Can you find?

1 melting moon

2 black spaceships

3 beach balls

4 one-eyed sun visors

5 parasols

Hot, hot, hot!

This planet is scorchingly close to its sun and the temperature is nearly 1,000°F! Can you find all the things listed?

6 space cocktails

7 pool floats

8 ice pops

9 dead bugs

10 jars of alien eyes

Alien escape

Uh-oh! All kinds of the worst, most troublesome aliens have escaped from the space station prison. Can you find all the things listed?

Can you find?

1 governor's portrait

2 space cats

3 furry aliens

4 red aliens

5 aliens with claws

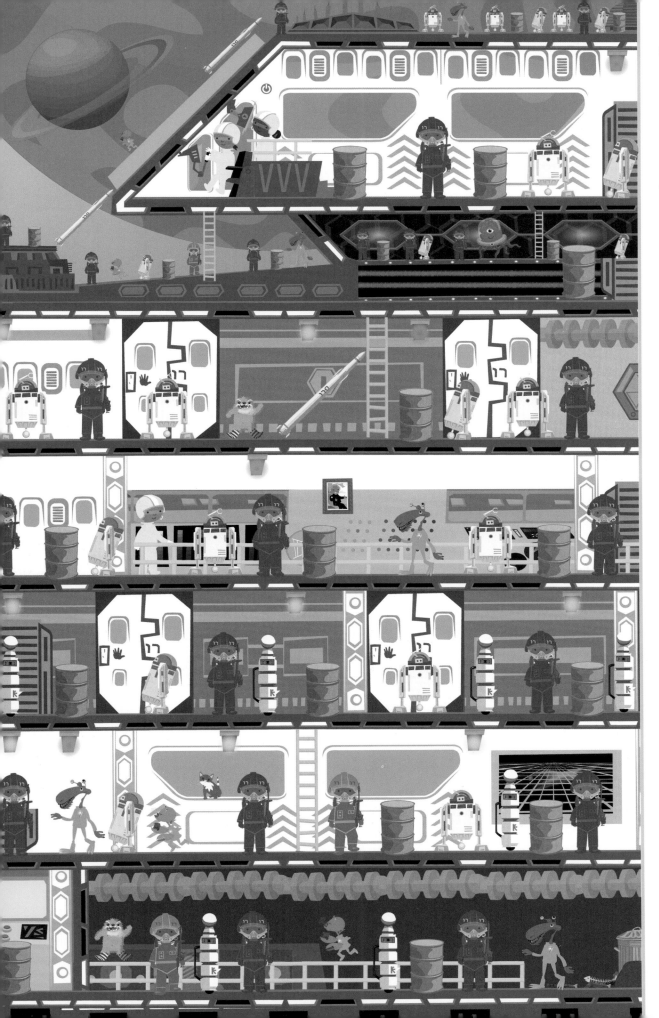

Can you find?

6 missiles

7 blue guards

8 ladders

9 aliens like this

10 red lights

1 tuba

2 spacecraft

3 Venus flytraps

4 tablet computers

5 space crabs

Crazy class

It's time for school for these young aliens, but some of them are not behaving! Can you find all the things listed?

Can you find?

6 balls
of paper

7 open
books

8 paper
airplanes

9 flowerpots

10 marbles

Can you find?

1 orange planet

2 two-headed snakes

3 helicopters

4 cranes

5 airplanes

Alien cousins

This planet is the most similar to Earth and the aliens who live here are suspiciously like human beings. But something's not quite right! Can you find all the things listed?

Can you find?

6 briefcases

7 chip packets

8 firefighters

9 milkshakes

10 pineapples

Can you find?

**1
Stegosaurus**

**2
Diplodocus**

**3
Allosaurus**

**4
Triceratops**

**5 alien
spacecraft**

Dinosaurs in space

Although dinosaurs became extinct on Earth millions of years ago, on this planet they are still alive and well. Can you find all the things listed?

Can you find?

6 moon buggies

7 drones

8 Pterodactyls

9 Coelophysis

10 Iguanodon

Can you find?

1 spaceship

2 brown mugs

3 red aliens

4 pairs of crutches

5 weird green sponges

Alien sickbay

At this space hospital, the doctors never know what kind of problem they'll see, or even what species! Can you find all the things listed?

Can you find?

6 bottles of potion

7 machines like this

8 furry aliens

9 bedpans

10 dead bugs

Can you find?

1 spaceship like this

2 yellow moons

3 green robots

4 spaceships like this

5 miners with scanners

Mine craft

The natural resources on Earth ran out long ago. This mining craft searches the universe for precious metals and minerals. Can you find all the things listed?